THERE'S A
DRAGON
IN MY
BACKPACK!

by TOM NICOLL

Illustrated by
SARAH HORNE

tiger tales

For my grandma, missed every day,
and my grandpa, who I blame for
making me a reader—T.N.

For Pops—S.H.

tiger tales

5 River Road, Suite 128, Wilton, CT 06897
Published in the United States 2019
Originally published in Great Britain 2017 by the Little Tiger Group
Text copyright © 2017 Tom Nicoll
Illustrations copyright © 2017 Sarah Horne
ISBN-13: 978-1-68010-445-5
ISBN-10: 1-68010-445-4
Printed in China
STP/1800/0249/0219
10 9 8 7 6 5 4 3 2 1

For more insight and activities, visit us at www.tigertalesbooks.com

Contents

Chapter 1
BRING YOUR DRAGON TO SCHOOL DAY
5

Chapter 2
NEW TOBY
28

Chapter 3
BRING YOUR DRAGON TO SCHOOL DAY: TAKE TWO
47

Chapter 4
GONE DRAGON GONE
55

Chapter 5
THE BREAKOUT
64

Chapter 6
WELCOME TO LA-DI-DA LAND
77

Chapter 7
FISHING FOR DRAGONS
91

Chapter 8
SHOWDOWN
105

Chapter 9
THE RETURN TRIP
112

Chapter 10
ROAR AND TELL
126

CHAPTER 1

BRING YOUR DRAGON TO SCHOOL DAY

There's a dragon in my backpack. This is what I've been reminding myself of all day.

Q. Why is there a dragon in my backpack?

A. Because I'm too nice, that's why!
And because the dragon's right—it's not fair that he has to stay in my bedroom all day.

Q. Why is there a dragon living in my bedroom?

A. Oh yeah, sorry. I should explain. . . .

The dragon isn't one of those full-sized, princess-stealing, knight-guzzling dragons that you've probably heard of. For one thing, I'd never fit one of those in my bag. No, he's a Mini-Dragon. Which means he looks exactly like one of those other dragons—same green scaly skin, fiery breath, sharp teeth and claws—except that he's about 6 inches tall and can talk. Oh, can he talk! His name is Pan, and here's how he came into my life:

Property developers destroy Pan's home in China.

Pan's parents bundle him in a crate of bean sprouts bound for Mexico to stay with his aunt and uncle.

BRING YOUR DRAGON TO SCHOOL DAY

The restaurant in Mexico that ordered
the bean sprouts closes down.
The crate is sent to the United States, to
my friend Min's parents' Chinese restaurant.

Min delivers Pan to my
house in a takeout meal
without realizing.

I end up with a Mini-Dragon
who constantly gives me grief.

So now Pan spends most of his day in my house playing video games, reading comics, and watching TV. Which sounds like a perfect day to me, but for some reason, he finds it boring. For a while now, he's been begging me to let him come to school, and last night I finally gave in, on the condition that he keep quiet and stay out of sight in my bag.

Surprisingly, today has actually been going well. Aside from the odd whisper from Pan, asking me to repeat something he missed or helpfully providing me with the answer to an addition problem or 10, he's kept his word. And it's almost time to go home now, so I can probably stop worrying. I mean, realistically, there's almost no chance at all of something going wrong....

"RAAAAAAAAAAAAAAAAT!"

Almost no chance.

That screaming woman who looks a bit like a yeti is Miss Biggs, my teacher. She thinks she's just seen a rat run across the classroom floor.

She hasn't.

She's just seen a Mini-Dragon run across the classroom floor.

Although completely different, I can see why she might confuse the two. If you had just caught sight of a tiny creature darting across the room, you'd probably think rat before you thought Mini-Dragon. To be honest, you'd probably never think Mini-Dragon.

Unless you happen to be me. In which case you'd *always* think Mini-Dragon.

As screaming kids began to barge their way to the door, I noticed Miss Biggs reaching under her desk and pulling out the tennis racket everyone knows she keeps there. No one quite knows what it's for, although there have been plenty of gruesome stories passed down over the years about Miss Biggs using it on misbehaving kids, annoying parents, and even the odd unruly teacher. No one really believes the stories, of course, but then no one thinks she plays tennis with it, either.

"Um…. Miss Biggs, what's that for?" I asked, swallowing a huge lump in my throat.

"This is Doris," smiled Miss Biggs, thumping the racket in her hand. "And Doris doesn't take kindly to vermin in her classroom. Doris gets very angry. And when Doris gets angry, things get smashed."

Miss Biggs was considered the toughest teacher around thanks to her enormous, muscle-bound physique and general bad attitude. In fact, people liked to imagine what Miss Biggs might have done before she became an evil, heartless school teacher. These theories included:

A championship boxer who was forced to retire when no one would fight her any more—not even the men.

A commando who was chucked out of the forces for being too rough with the other soldiers.

A crash-test dummy before crash-test dummies were invented.

The person at the zoo whose job it is to step in whenever any of the animals start fighting.

With her massive head of curly white hair, Miss Biggs has always reminded me of a yeti. You might think that's funny, but trust me, a yeti armed with a tennis racket is no laughing matter.

Anyway, where was I? Oh, yeah—my

escaped Mini-Dragon. "Jayden, where are you going?" I said, grabbing the arm of my best friend as he ran past me alongside hoards of fleeing kids.

Jayden looked at me as if I had lost my mind. "Where do you think I'm going?" he said. "I'm getting away from the rat."

"Ha, you're such a chicken," said Min, our other friend, calmly staying put.

It occurred to me that since Min had been the one to bring Pan into my life, technically this was all her fault. But I just had to try those free bean sprouts, didn't I?

"It's not a rat," I whispered, trying to remain calm on the outside, while on the inside I was getting very worried about the thought of Miss Biggs squashing our little friend. "It's *Pan.*"

"Of course it is," groaned Min.

"A pan won't be any use against a rat,"

said Miss Biggs, twirling her racket in the air. "They're clever little beasts—cleverer than all of you, that's for sure. But not as clever as Doris and me." She paused. "What was that?"

Miss Biggs spun around and swung the racket like a hammer, smashing an entire desk in two. Jayden, Min, and I, the only kids left in the room, let out a huge gasp.

Fortunately, there was no sign of Pan in the wreckage.

"Phew," I said.

Miss Biggs scowled in frustration. "Thought for sure I saw it there." She turned and glared at us. "If you three are sticking around, make yourselves useful. Find that rat! Flush it out."

We nodded. Finding Pan before Miss Biggs did seem like a good idea.

As Miss Biggs stalked around the classroom, Jayden began checking under desks, and Min started looking in cupboards. I scanned the room, trying to think of the likeliest place Pan would be. Then it dawned on me. I headed toward the storage trays and pulled out the one with my name on it.

"Oh, hey, Eric," whispered Pan. He was sitting in the tray, clutching a piece of paper, trying to look as casual as possible—as if this was a perfectly normal place for me to find him. "How's it going?"

Mini-Dragons, in their own words, are excellent at a lot of things, but acting innocent isn't one of them.

"We had a deal," I whispered back. "Escaping from my backpack to have a look in this tray was *not* part of it."

Pan looked at me doubtfully. "It wasn't?"

"No!"

"I'm not so sure," he said slowly. "It's a bit of a gray area, isn't it?"

I looked at Pan in amazement. "How is it a gray area?" I asked. "I said, 'stay in the bag.' You came out of the bag. That's not gray. That's black … or white…. But it's definitely not gray."

"Well, look," said Pan, trying to sound reasonable. "It's clear that neither one of us is right, so I think we should just forget the whole thing and move on."

I glanced over my shoulder to check that Miss Biggs hadn't seen us, but she and Doris were busy threatening a flower pot at the other end of the room. "Why did you escape?" I asked.

BRING YOUR DRAGON TO SCHOOL DAY

"It was so boring inside that bag," Pan grumbled. "And so, so hot—I mean, I know I'm a dragon and should be used to high temperatures, but still! Anyway, I've just been taking a look through some of your drawings. Is this supposed to be me? I mean, I'm flattered you drew me. But you have to admit, it looks nothing like me. You haven't captured my good looks at all."

"Crisp!" bellowed Miss Biggs from across the room. "Who are you talking to? Not the rat, I hope! There's no reasoning with rats, Crisp. Stand back. Doris is coming through."

I spun around, the color draining from my face. I had to think fast. I took a step backward, quickly banging the drawer shut with my bum, causing Pan to let out a little yelp. As Miss Biggs thundered toward us, I pointed at the door.

"Out there, Miss Biggs," I said. "I just saw it heading into the hallway."

Miss Biggs screeched to a halt. "You're sure?" she asked.

"I think I saw it, too," said Min, who seemed to realize what I was doing.

"Yeah," said Jayden, giving me a wink to show he understood. "It was huge. Had a big smile on its face."

"Thinks it's gotten away from me, does it?"

said Miss Biggs. "Come on, Doris, let's go and show that rat how wrong it is."

As soon as Miss Biggs left the room, I pulled out the tray. Pan was sitting there, his claws covering his mouth, looking like he was about to barf.

"What's wrong?" I asked him.

"I found some prawn crackers in your tray," he groaned, "but they tasted horrible."

I scratched my head. There weren't any prawn crackers in my tray. There were just some drawings and…. Oh!

"Pan," I said. "Those prawn crackers. They weren't glued to a piece of paper in the shape of a face, were they?"

A groggy-looking Pan nodded weakly.

"Those were Styrofoam chips," I said. "We used them in art last week."

Pan let out a belch, and a jet of flame came out after it.

"Ooh, that's much better," said Pan.

"Not really," I said as the flame caught one of my drawings. Pan quickly leaped into my arms. Min moved fast, grabbing a jug of water from Miss Biggs's desk and throwing it over the tray.

The pictures were ruined, but at least the fire was out.

As Min swiftly returned the jug to Miss Biggs's desk, Jayden and I opened the window and started wafting out the smoke before the alarm could go off. When I was sure we were in the clear, I quickly closed it again and turned back to Pan. He grinned at me apologetically, but I'd had enough.

"Now, stay out of sight," I said, bundling him into my bag. "Or you'll be the first Mini-Dragon to make a home-run—as the ball."

"But that's baseball," said Pan.

"Yeah, he's right," said Jayden.

"It'd be serving an ace in tennis," added Min.

"Fine," I said, rolling my eyes. "My point is he'd be on the wrong end of a tennis racket." I glared at Pan. "If you're cool with that, then you're welcome to stay out."

I waited for a response but was greeted with silence. "That's what I thought," I said, zipping up my bag.

Ten minutes later, Miss Biggs burst back into the classroom, a foul look on her face.

"Get back in here, everyone!" she shouted. The rest of the class hurried in from the hallway as fast as they had left.

An awkward silence filled the room.

"Did you get it, Miss Biggs?" asked Jayden.

Min and I shook our heads in disbelief. Of course she hadn't gotten it. There was nothing to get!

"No, I didn't," snapped Miss Biggs. "I thought I had it, but … well … to make a long story short, we no longer have a functioning coffee machine in the staff room."

Miss Biggs had barely sat down at her desk before another scowl appeared on her face. "What happened to my water?" she roared. "Which one of you is responsible for this?"

Min, Jayden, and I glanced at each other with panicked expressions. I couldn't tell Miss Biggs who was actually responsible, not unless I wanted a flattened Mini-Dragon.

I put up my hand. "It was me, Miss Biggs," I said. "I got thirsty."

Min and Jayden looked at me in horror. They knew I was in for it now. I could see them both starting to raise their hands. They were going to take the blame with me. I gave them a look that said, "Don't do it, there's no point in all three of us getting in trouble." They seemed to get the message and lowered their hands, though neither of them looked very happy about it.

"The entire jug?" said Miss Biggs, looking flabbergasted. "This is *my* water, Crisp. *Mine.* You can think about that when you're writing me a 500-word report on the history of rats."

"That's not fair," I said.

"Not fair?" repeated Miss Biggs. "No, Crisp, not fair is me knowing that somewhere out there is a rat who escaped justice. And now I can't even have a drink of my own water—*that's* not fair!"

I sighed, slumping in my chair. *Could this day get any worse?* I thought to myself.

Which was a mistake. Of course it could get worse.

"Oh, and Crisp?"

"Yes, Miss Biggs?"

"Have it on my desk by tomorrow morning."

With Miss Biggs, it always got worse.

CHAPTER 2
NEW TOBY

"Hey, Toby," I said as I got out of the car later that day. He was climbing out of his parents' huge car next door and did not look happy. I mean, he never does, that's just Toby, but today he looked especially *un*happy. He was still wearing his P.E. uniform, which might have explained his mood—Toby hated exercise. He completely ignored me, dragging his bag by the straps into his house and slamming the door behind him.

Here's a picture of Toby's backpack, by the way:

NEW TOBY

Toby's backpack

And here's one
of mine:

Look familiar? I had mine for a whole
day before Toby made his mom buy him
the same one. He hates it if I ever have
something he doesn't. Even worse, afterward
he insists that I copied him.

"Well, that was nice," I said, staring at

Toby's closed front door.

"Oh, he mustn't have heard you," said Mom as she unhooked my little sister Posy from her car seat. "Don't worry; he'll be coming over for dinner tonight, so you can catch up with him then."

"Woo-hoo!" I said sarcastically.

"Of course you can't come back to school," I told Pan once we were in my room, stunned that he would even bother to ask.

"Awww," he moaned, as he climbed out of my bag. "But it's soooo boring being stuck in the house all day."

"If you think that's boring, then you've obviously never had to write a report for Miss Biggs before," I said.

Pan looked confused. "Of course I haven't. I'm a Mini-Dragon."

"Yes, I know, I meant.... Oh, never mind," I said. "Look, we tried it today, and it was a disaster."

"But next time, I promise—"

"No, Pan," I said, putting my foot down. "Look, I'd better go. Toby's coming over for dinner."

Pan folded his tiny arms, the clear beginnings of a Mini-Dragon sulk.

"Don't be like that," I said. I undid the front pocket of my backpack and took out a paper bag. "Look, Min gave me some prawn crackers."

Mini-Dragons love prawn crackers almost as much as they love dirty laundry. In fact, according to the *Encyclopaedia Dragonica*, a huge book containing everything you could ever want to know about dragons, Mini-Dragons actually only have three main food groups:

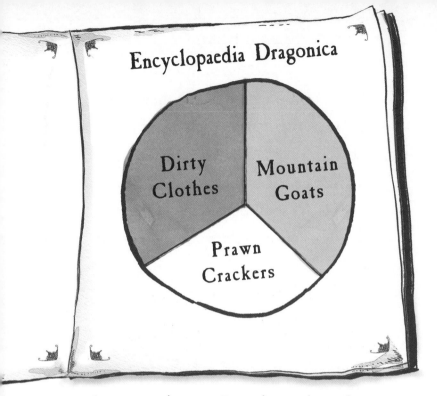

Encyclopaedia Dragonica

Dirty Clothes

Mountain Goats

Prawn Crackers

I try to make sure Pan always has plenty of prawn crackers around so that I don't have to explain to Mom why my school clothes look like they lost a fight with a cactus.

Without even a glance in my direction, Pan snatched the bag, then retreated to a corner of the bed. With his back to me, he began munching away. I left him to it.

When I walked into the kitchen, Dad was sitting at the table as Mom served dinner—lasagna. The only good thing about Toby coming over for dinner was that Mom always made her best dishes.

"Where's Toby?" I asked, looking around. Nothing made me more nervous than seeing food with Toby's name on it and not seeing Toby. It was a sure sign of trouble.

"It's not like him to be late," said Mom.

DIIIIIIIIIIING-DONGGGGGG!

"That should be him now," said Dad.

"Eric, go and let him in," said Mom.

I opened the door. Sure enough it was Toby, but not the Toby I knew.

"Good evening, Eric!" he said, which set off more alarm bells. There were a total of three things wrong with that sentence:

1. Toby never greeted anyone. The closest he normally came was a half-hearted grunt.

2. He had used my actual name. Not "Crispo," "You," "Goofball," "Pain," or "Trouble."

3. It was said with a smile. I've seen Toby smirk tons of times and he has a pretty impressive nasty grin that he likes to roll out on special occasions, but I've never seen him do a proper smile before. It was creepy.

"What are you up to?" I said, narrowing my eyes.

"What do you mean?" he asked innocently.

"If I didn't know better, I'd almost think you were trying to be nice," I said as we headed for the kitchen.

"What *are* you going on about, Eric?" said Toby, letting me enter the room first. "I'm *always* nice. Hello, Mrs. Crisp, Mr. Crisp."

"Um … hello, Toby," said my parents, looking as confused as me.

"Ooh, lasagna," said Toby, clapping his hands. "How wonderful."

Mom and Dad turned toward me as if expecting some kind of explanation for Nice Toby, but all I could offer was a shrug. I had no idea who this boy was or what he had done with the real Toby.

"You're all looking well," said Toby.

It continued like this for the rest of the meal:

Your food is amazing, Mrs. Crisp, as always!

How was school, Eric?

You must give this delightful recipe to my mom. She won't use it herself, of course, but she'll pass it along to our cook.

How are the Kickers doing this season, Mr. Crisp? I must come along soon and lend my support.

NEW TOBY

"Huh?" I said. I had heard the words, but coming from Toby, my brain was having a difficult time making any sense of them. Toby didn't ask questions like this. Toby asked questions like:

Can you guess what my parents just bought me?

Is there any more?

Is that all I'm getting?

Are you going to finish that?

Why are you so clueless, Crispo?

"Toby's asking you how school was, dear,"
said Mom slowly, as if she couldn't quite
believe what she was saying.

Dad was just staring at Toby in amazement,
his mouth wide open.

"Um … fine," I said. Of course it hadn't
been fine, but I could barely remember
school at that point, I was so confused.

"It's show-and-tell tomorrow, isn't it, Eric?" said Mom.

"Oh, we have that, too," said Toby.

(Toby and I don't go to the same school. I go to Deerfield Elementary, and Toby goes to the Lexington Academy for the Development and Improvement of the Deeply Advantaged. Toby calls it Lexington. To everyone else it's the La-Di-Da.

I don't know that much about the La-Di-Da really, except that it's expensive to go there, and they have just about everything you could ever think of, like their own football stadium and a safari park and a private airfield. At least that's what Toby says. I'm not sure he's always truthful about his school. Jayden is convinced that all the kids who go there are exactly like Toby, which isn't worth thinking about.)

"So, what are you showing?" continued

Toby. "Not the Mini-Drag—"

"No," I said, cutting him off. Mom and Dad do know about Pan, but what they know is different than what Toby knows. In fact, it was getting so hard to keep track of who believed what that I ended up creating this handy pocket chart:

PERSON(S)	WHAT THEY THINK PAN IS
Mom/Dad	A toy Jayden gave me for my ninth birthday
Toby	A super-advanced toy with state-of-the-art artificial intelligence and awesome fire-breathing abilities
Patches	Prey
Posy	A teething toy
Min/Jayden	An actual Mini-Dragon

The first time Toby ever saw Pan, I told him he was a new toy. Pan had frozen at the time—a defense mechanism that Mini-Dragons have when they sense danger—so it wasn't that hard to convince him. Since then, Toby has witnessed Pan talking and moving, yet somehow it still hasn't occurred to him that Pan isn't battery-operated.

Yeah, he's not that bright.

"I'm doing my show-and-tell with Min and Jayden," I replied. "We're showing the walkie-talkies we've been using recently."

"Walkie-talkies?" said Toby, looking unimpressed. "Why don't you just use your cell phones? Mine lets you video chat with a hundred people at the same time. And you can play Penguin Ninja on it."

"Eric doesn't have a cell phone," said Mom.

Toby looked at her as if she had just spoken a foreign language.

"The range on the walkie-talkies is amazing," I said. "Up to three miles."

Toby shook his head in bewilderment. "My phone has a range of the entire planet."

Wow, I thought, *finally something I have that Toby doesn't want.* Although, in this case, only because he has something better.

"So, what are you taking to your show-and-tell, Toby?" asked Dad.

Toby shifted uncomfortably in his chair. "Well, that's still up in the air at the moment. Actually, Eric, about that…. Could I have a word? In private?"

"I can't chat for long—I've got a report due tomorrow," I said as we entered the living room. "Can we forget about video games for now?"

Toby looked around distractedly. "What? Oh, right, yeah, fine, whatever. Listen, since you're not using that dragon ... can I borrow it for a bit? Please? Only for a day, I promise."

Somehow I managed to avoid laughing in Toby's face. He had already stolen Pan once before; the chances of me voluntarily handing Pan over to him were about the same as Toby being awarded a Nobel Prize for Honesty.

But still, I was curious. "What do you need him for?" I asked.

"You have no idea what show-and-tell is like at Lexington," said Toby. "These are the most privileged kids in the country. Showing off their things is like an Olympic sport to them. If you don't have something amazing that no one else has, then the other kids humiliate you."

"I'm sure it's not that bad…," I said.

Toby flopped onto the couch, holding his head in his hands. "It is!" he said. "They made a kid cry last month because he brought in a solid gold watch."

"Wow," I said, impressed. "What was wrong with that?"

"It was from last season!"

I shook my head in amazement. "Well … I'm sure you have plenty of cool things you could show them."

"I have plenty of cool things I could show *you*," said Toby, rolling his eyes, "but not *them*. Please, Crispo—I mean, Eric, I need your help. I've searched the internet trying to find a dragon myself, but it's like they don't exist. Did you get yours delivered?"

I nodded, hiding a smile, and decided against telling Toby that Pan had arrived in a Chinese takeout box.

44

Toby put his hands together, his face pleading like a puppy. "Please, Eric, I'm desperate," he said.

"I can see that," I said, realizing how hard it must be for Toby to beg like this. "But I'm sorry, the answer is no."

Toby's face almost exploded with rage. "I knew you'd be no help! I can't believe I was actually nice to you. And your parents. Your mom's cooking is garbage, by the way."

Toby stormed out of the house, leaving me alone in the living room with my mouth open.

"What was all that about?" asked Pan, popping out from behind the couch.

"I have no idea," I said, smiling down at him. "How long have you been there?"

"Long enough to know that boy is still crazy," said Pan.

I nodded. "Oh, well, at least I'll have some peace to work on the report that I'm never going to finish for tomorrow. Five hundred words in one night! It's impossible."

Pan folded his tiny arms and leaned confidently against the couch. "Funny you should say that," he said, "because you'll never guess what Mini-Dragons happen to be excellent at...."

CHAPTER 3

BRING YOUR DRAGON TO SCHOOL DAY: TAKE TWO

The following morning, Dad had left for work, and I was outside waiting by the car for Mom and Posy when my backpack began to crackle.

I opened the zipper a little and peered in. "Pan," I said. "Switch off the walkie-talkie."

"Oops, sorry," the Mini-Dragon replied. "I was just checking that it still works."

"Please don't," I said. "You'll use up the battery. And remember the deal: you helped me with my report, so I'm bringing you to school again. But this time, you need

47

to stay in my backpack—no more breaks for freedom. And you need to stay quiet. I don't mean your usual *noisy* quiet. I mean *really* quiet this time."

"Ah," said Pan. "You mean *quiet* quiet. All right, gotcha."

"Good," I said.

"You won't hear a peep from me all day," said Pan.

"Thank you," I said.

"Not a word."

"Right," I said.

"Total silence."

"Okay...."

"Complete and utter—"

"Pan!"

"All right, all right," said Pan. "No more talking, starting ... now."

I zipped up my bag and put it down on the ground while I enjoyed the silence, which only lasted for a few seconds. But this time it wasn't Pan's fault.

"All right, Crispo?"

I burst out laughing.

"BWAAHAHAHAHA!"

Toby frowned. "Ugh. Every morning's the same with you. As soon as I show up, you start laughing. But I never see anything funny, and you never tell me what the joke is."

"Heh … I'm sorry, Toby," I said, wiping a tear from my eye. "I don't know what's wrong with me."

"I could write you a list," grumbled Toby.

The truth was, I knew *exactly* what made me laugh every day. It was the sight of Toby in his La-Di-Da uniform, which consisted of:

1. A ketchup-red and mustard-yellow pinstripe jacket and matching tie over a gray shirt.

2. Gray shorts that don't even reach the knees. They do have special winter shorts that are an extra two inches longer, though.

3. A red lapel flower.

4. A straw hat with a red ribbon around it. The height of your hat was determined by your age. Toby was nine, so his hat was nine inches high. It was basically a wicker top hat at this stage.

5. Gray socks, black shoes. There's actually nothing funny about them, I just mention them in case you worry that La-Di-Da children have to go to school barefoot. The outfit is crazy, but it's not that crazy.

All in all, it was a little more extravagant than our plain red sweater, black pants, white shirt, and gray-and-black tie.

"Don't suppose you've changed your mind about that dragon toy?" asked Toby.

I shook my head. "Sorry."

"What a surprise," he muttered.

"So what are you taking to show-and-tell instead?" I asked.

"What?" said Toby, barely listening. "Oh, Dad got me some book.... Charlie Dickens's *Great Expeditions* or something."

"You mean … *Great Expectations*?" I asked. "Dad has that one. I think he said it was pretty good."

Toby snorted. "Hardly! It's ancient. Who's going to be impressed by some old book? Dad keeps going on about it being a first edition and to be careful with it, but honestly, it's all brown and horrible-looking. If you ask me, I'd be doing him a favor to throw it away so he can get himself a new one."

"Um … I wouldn't do that," I said.

"Whatever," mumbled Toby. "It's not like I've got anything better to show … thanks to you."

"ERRRRRIIIICCCCC!" shouted Mom from the house.

"Uh-oh, I better go," I said. I ran back

inside to find Mom on the kitchen floor with her feet pinning her arms to the back of her head. Posy, a purple crayon stuffed in her mouth, and our cat, Patches, were sitting watching her like she was putting on some kind of show.

"Um...," said Mom, her face looking a bit flushed. "I had an idea for my yoga class this morning, but I don't think it's going to work. You couldn't give me a hand, could you?" I untied Mom, and she let out a sigh of relief. "Ah, that's better. Thanks, Eric." She scooped Posy up in her arms. "Okay, everyone out ... now. Not you, Patches."

We rushed out and got into the car. As I strapped myself in, I heard a tapping sound and looked up to see Toby knocking on the window. I pressed the button to open it.

"Forgetting something?" said Toby, holding up my bag.

My stomach dropped. "Oh, no!" I said, pulling the bag into the car. "Thanks, Toby."

Toby smiled the same way he had been smiling the night before. "No problem, Eric. Anything for my good friend!"

I frowned. "All right, Toby, you can drop the nice-guy act. The answer is still no. I'm sure your show-and-tell will go just fine without the dragon."

Toby nodded, still smiling. "Oh, I'm sure you're right, Eric. Best of luck for yours, too. Have a great day!"

Baffled, I shook my head and watched him waving as we drove off, before Mom switched the CD player on and launched into her daily playlist of terrible show-tunes. To his credit, I didn't hear a peep out of Pan for the entire journey.

I should have known then that something was wrong.

CHAPTER 4

GONE DRAGON GONE

"Report, Crisp," barked Miss Biggs before I had even sat down in class.

"Yes, Miss Biggs," I said. I opened my backpack carefully, just in case Pan forgot where he was and sprung out. But he didn't.

I reached into the bag for the folder I had put the report in—Miss Biggs hated crumpled homework. As I fumbled around, I was overcome by a sinking feeling in the pit of my stomach. Had I left the folder at home?

Then my hand fell on something I didn't

recognize. Something hard and leathery. Not leathery like a Mini-Dragon—leathery like an old book. A very old book.

I pulled on the zipper, opening the bag up completely. There wasn't much inside—a pencil case, a couple of workbooks, and an old-looking copy of *Great Expectations* by Charles Dickens.

No report. And no Pan. Pan being quiet had been a clue something was wrong, but I realized that I'd missed an even bigger one—Toby being nice. He must have switched our bags while I was helping Mom. Which meant ... Toby had Pan.

I had never felt so ill in all my life.

"What's wrong, Crisp?" asked Miss Biggs with mock concern. "Forgot your report, by any chance?"

I opened my mouth, but nothing came out. I nodded.

"Oh, dear," she said, not even bothering to hide her delight. "What a surprise. Don't worry, Crisp. You'll have plenty of time to finish it—in lunchtime detention."

I couldn't wait to talk to Min and Jayden at recess and explain what had happened.

"Oh, no!" gasped Min, covering her mouth with her hands. "Poor Pan."

"I can't believe that thieving Toby," said Jayden. "Well ... actually, I can. This is *exactly* the sort of thing he'd do."

"I can't believe I left my bag outside," I said.

THERE'S A **DRAGON** IN MY **BACKPACK!**

"Eric, you shouldn't blame yourself," said Min. "Although, obviously, it was your fault."

"Um … thanks, Min," I said. "That made me feel a whole lot better."

Suddenly, I heard a familiar-sounding crackle.

"What's that?" I said, looking around.

"It's my walkie-talkie," said Jayden. "Didn't realize I still had it on."

"Switch it off," said Min. "You'll waste the battery. We only have two walkie-talkies to show now and if yours doesn't work, what am I supposed to do?"

Jayden thought about it. "You could talk to yourself."

Min rolled her eyes.

"Fine, but I can't believe you're worried about battery life at a time like this," said Jayden, taking the walkie-talkie out of his pocket. He was just about to click the off-switch when we heard a familiar voice.

"Eric … are you there? Eric, over?"

"PAN!" shouted the three of us at once, which got us some funny looks from the other kids in the playground.

"Eric, is that you, over?" asked Pan.

"Yes, Pan, it's me," I said. "Min and Jayden are here, too. Where are you?"

There was silence at the other end.

"Pan, are you still there?" I asked eventually.

"Oh, yeah, sorry," said Pan. "I thought you hadn't finished talking—you didn't say 'over' like in that cop film I watched last week when you were in school. Over."

I let out a sigh. "Pan, don't worry about saying 'over.' Just tell me where you are."

"I'm in your bag," said Pan, "but I don't think I'm at your school. For one thing, Toby is here."

"He switched the backpacks, Pan," said Jayden.

"Yeah, that's what I figured," said Pan, his voice trembling a little. "Mini-Dragons are excellent at knowing when they've been dragon-napped."

"Is Toby there right now?" I asked, trying to stop my own voice from wobbling. I wasn't going to help Pan by sounding scared. Even though I definitely was.

"No," said Pan. "He's doing pee-wee at the moment."

The three of us looked at each other blankly. "He's in the bathroom?" I asked.

"No, *pee-wee*," said Pan. "You know … sports."

"Oh," I said. "You mean P.E.?"

"That's what I said," said Pan.

Jayden looked confused. "Wait … are you telling me Toby actually plays sports? That's like finding out Miss Biggs is human."

I ignored him. "Pan, about Toby's show-and-tell—" I began.

"That's not happening until 12," interrupted Pan. "I heard Toby and some other boys talking about it."

"Twelve?" said Min. "At lunchtime?"

"No, they have lunch later than us," I said. "Everything's different at La-Di-Da's. Hang on, Pan—I'm coming to get you."

"*We're* coming to get you," corrected Min.

"We are?" said Jayden. "Um … I mean … we *are*! But when are we going to be able to sneak out?"

"Lunchtime," I said.

"But you've got detention with Miss Biggs," said Min.

"Not to mention that La-Di-Da is miles away," added Jayden.

"There has to be a way," I said. "We can't let Toby show Pan to his classmates. Anyone with half a brain will figure out he's not a toy. He could end up locked away in a laboratory with mad scientists experimenting on him all day. I'm sure Toby said that La-Di-Da have their own science labs—they'll probably just take him there. We might never see him again."

"Eric's right," said Min. "A lot of the kids at

Toby's school are smart."

"I dunno," said Jayden, looking unconvinced. "They can't be *that* smart if they agree to wear that uniform."

But I wasn't really listening anymore. I was trying to come up with a plan. And I had nothing.

CHAPTER 5
THE BREAKOUT

By the time lunchtime rolled around, I still had nothing.

"Have a seat, Crisp," said Miss Biggs, who seemed to be taking great delight in my punishment. Well, at least one of us was having a good time.

"Just you and me today," she said, slamming her legs onto her desk and leaning back in her comfy leather chair. "Which means you have my entire focus. So don't even think about trying to get something past me, Crisp. I've got eyes like a hawk. A hawk carrying binoculars, in fact. And I have eyes in the back of my head, too."

"Normal eyes or hawk eyes?" I asked, slightly confused.

"Hawk eyes," said Miss Biggs.

"So how many eyes do you have in total?"

"What? No, look, I have two eyes—two actual eyes—but they're very good, and they see all around."

"Like … an owl?" I suggested.

Miss Biggs thought about this. "Yes, a little like an owl. So I'm an owl and a hawk. Clear?"

"Not really," I said.

"Look, it's— Oh, never mind. Get that report written and no more talking."

"Yes, Miss Biggs."

I stared at the blank piece of paper on the desk in front of me, but all I could think about was what might be happening to Pan.

Or what would happen to him if we couldn't get him back. I suddenly had a vision of Pan trapped inside a glass box. He looked terrified, tears running down his snout.

I shook my head to try and get rid of the image. I had to get out of here. But how?

A plan began to formulate in my mind:

1. I pretend that I have to use the bathroom.

2. Because she's horrible, Miss Biggs says no and that I should have gone earlier.

3. I tell her I'll burst if I don't go.

4. Thinking only of the mess that would be made, she lets me go, but accompanies me and waits outside the bathroom.

5. I climb out of a window.

6. Miss Biggs realizes I'm gone and chases after me. So I commandeer a car to escape.

7. She has her own car, so it's a high-speed car chase through town. Rather than head for La-Di-Da, I take a detour toward the local airforce base, where I crash through the barriers and then on to a runway.

8. I drive alongside a fighter jet getting ready to take off, then jump on to it, overpower the pilot, knock him out, and then take control of the plane myself.

9. Miss Biggs tries to catch up in an Apache helicopter, but I take her out with a couple of heat-seeking rockets.

10. I arrive at La-Di-Da, where I blow the roof off whatever building Pan is in before dropping a rope for him to grab hold of. Then I fly us both home. EASY.

THE BREAKOUT

I was about to raise my hand when I realized that my master plan wouldn't be required after all.

It turns out Miss Biggs *is* like an owl. They both like to sleep during the day.

It was a pity. I was really looking forward to flying that fighter jet.

"Wow, you made it," said Jayden as I arrived at the school's front gate where we'd arranged to meet. "How did you manage that?"

"Oh, I have my ways," I said, giving him a wry smile.

"Snoring her head off, isn't she?" said Jayden.

I frowned. "How do you know that?"

"I had detention with her a couple of months ago," said Jayden. "She slept through the entire lunch period."

"Let's hope she does the same today! Where's Min?" I asked.

Jayden shrugged. "She told me to wait here—she wanted to check something."

I looked at my watch. "We can't wait for long," I said.

"Pan, are you there?" I said, taking the

70

walkie-talkie from Jayden.

"Yeah, I'm here," said Pan. He sounded panicked. "I think show-and-tell is about to start. I've unzipped the zipper on your bag a little so I can see what's going on. We're in some kind of hall. And there's a stage. There are tons of kids sitting around, waiting."

"A stage?" said Jayden. "Wow, they really take show-and-tell seriously over there."

"Pan, be careful that Toby doesn't hear us talking," I said, keeping my voice low.

"Not much chance of that," said Pan. "Toby's too busy telling everyone about how awesome his presentation is going to be, and it's so noisy with all the other kids anyway. I think the whole school is here."

"Not the *whole* school," said Min, appearing behind us.

"Min," I said, relieved to see her. "Where have you been?"

"Speaking to Danny Thirteentrees," she said with a grin. "He and the rest of the school soccer team are just getting ready to leave. They have a big game this afternoon."

Jayden shrugged. "And?"

"*And…*," said Min, "guess which posh school they happen to be playing!"

"You're kidding!" I said.

Min shook her head. "No, it's true—they're playing La-Di-Da! We have to be quick, though, because the bus is ready to leave."

"We're on our way, Pan," I said into the walkie-talkie. "If we don't make it in time to stop show-and-tell, I need you to pretend you're frozen, just like when we first met. Maybe they'll believe you're a toy, like I did."

"Okay, Eric, I will," said Pan, but I could tell from his small voice that he was worried.

THE BREAKOUT

The three of us sneaked into the back of the bus, hiding under a pile of what we hoped were clean soccer uniforms. Moments later, I could hear the sounds of an entire soccer team clambering on board.

"All right, everyone," said Mr. Waller, our P.E. teacher, as he started up the bus.

"Everyone here? Good, let's get going. We can't be late; La-Di-Da is strict about punctuality."

"It's true," said one of the boys. "I heard last week that they made Middleton forfeit for being 10 seconds late."

The bus lurched forward. We were on our way.

"Now, have you guys come up with a decent team name yet?" asked Mr. Waller.

"No," said Danny Thirteentrees. "Well, we've narrowed it down to the Deerfield Destroyers, the Deerfield Warriors, or the Deerfield Bears. But none of us can agree."

"What about the Deerfield *Dragons*?"

I recognized the voice. It was Pan. Beneath the soccer uniforms, I could see Min and Jayden's eyes bulging out of their sockets. My heart pounding, I fumbled in my pocket for the walkie-talkie. It was on monitor-mode–I must have accidentally leaned on it when we got into the bus. As I switched it off, I noticed that the entire bus had fallen silent.

The three of us lay there, expecting any moment to be caught.

But we weren't caught. Instead, Mr. Waller spoke. "I like it!" he said.

"Me, too," said Danny.

"*The Deerfield Dragons*. Has a nice ring to it."

I breathed a sigh of relief as a "Let's go, Dragons!" chant broke out among the team. It went on for a while. Just when I thought it was never going to end, the bus screeched to a halt.

"All right, Dragons, out you go," said Mr. Waller.

"Hey, look," shouted someone outside. "It's the Deerfield Dunces!"

"More like *Durr*field!" laughed another La-Di-Da student.

I could hear the doors opening and the team flooding out. "We're the Deerfield Dragons, actually!" declared Danny proudly.

As the two sides began to argue, we slipped out of the bus unnoticed. We sprinted toward the main building and hid behind a wall.

We had done it. We had made it to Toby's school.

Now for the *hard* part.

CHAPTER 6

WELCOME TO LA-DI-DA LAND

"Pan, we're outside," I hissed, switching the walkie-talkie back on.

"Hurry!" shouted Pan. "Show-and-tell has started, and I think it's almost Toby's turn. Right now there's a girl showing off a fishing rod, and it is *not* going well."

We could hear loud booing coming from the walkie-talkie.

"Tough crowd," said Min.

"Yeah, Toby wasn't joking when he said these kids were hard to please," I said. "All right, Pan, we're coming."

I looked around to try and figure out where we were. Then it dawned on me. This was a **BIG** school. Our school was a medium-sized, single-story building. Toby's school was more like a small town.

"It goes on for miles," said Jayden as our eyes followed the rows of grand, old-looking buildings. Turrets and spires jutted out everywhere. It was like being at a family reunion for castles.

"He could be anywhere," said Min.

"Pan, I don't suppose you know what building you're in, do you?" I said into the walkie-talkie.

"Yeah," said Pan. "I managed to sneak a peek. It's a big stone building, really old-looking, with a lot of pointy parts on the top."

I looked around again. "Every building looks like that," I said.

"Oh," said Pan. "Then I have no idea."

"Maybe we should split up and start checking all the buildings," suggested Min.

"That'll still take forever," said Jayden.

"I don't think we have any other option," I said.

BEEP-BEEEEPPPPP!

BEEP-BEEEEPPPPP!

The three of us spun on our heels. On the path in front of us was a freckle-faced boy sporting a huge grin. I could tell from the size of his hat that he was a little older than Toby, but it was what he was sitting in that really grabbed my attention.

A white, four-seater golf cart.

"Running late, are we?" he asked.

"Sorry?" said Jayden.

"For show-and-tell," he said. "I presume

that's where you're off to, dressed like that. I say, what odd outfits! I'm sure everyone will get quite a kick out of them."

An appalled Jayden looked the boy up and down. "*Our* outfits are odd?" he said.

"Yes, that's right, *they are*," I said quickly, giving Jayden a nod. "For show-and-tell—REMEMBER, Jayden?"

"Oh, right ... yeah," said Jayden, nodding back, though I'm not sure he knew why.

"Any chance of a lift?" asked Min.

"Of course," said the boy. "That *is* why they give these things to us seniors, after all—to keep the school running. Jump in."

"Thanks!" I said as the three of us climbed into the cart.

"The name's Roger," said the boy, shaking our hands. "Haven't seen you three before."

"We're new," lied Jayden. "We've just transferred here. These are the uniforms from our old school, you see. That's why we have them."

Roger nodded. "And are you all related?" he asked.

"Ha!" said Jayden. "Us? Related? Not likely!"

Roger looked confused. "So ... you're not related, but you all just transferred from the same school at exactly the same time?"

I could hear Min groaning next to me.

Jayden was a terrible liar, which is normally a good quality in a friend, but it wasn't helping us much here. His eyes were darting back and forth as he tried to find a way out of his lie. Eventually, he simply said:

"Yes."

Roger stared at him for a second before shrugging and turning back toward the path. "Okay. Alright, friends, hang on. She's a fast little thing."

He wasn't kidding. Roger pressed his foot down on the pedal, and the cart shot off along the path.

"I was just heading over to show-and-tell myself," he said over the noise of the cart. "I *was* planning on watching the soccer game, but then I heard about Toby Bloom. Have you met Toby yet?"

The three of us exchanged looks. "Yeah," I said. "We've met."

"Bit of an odd one, isn't he? Apparently he's been bragging all day that he's got something really impressive to show. Won't say what it is, though."

Roger put his foot down hard on the brake. The three of us flew out of the cart, landing in a heap.

"I told you to hang on," said Roger cheerfully, climbing out of his seat. "Everyone all right? Great! Anyway, here we are. I'll catch you inside. Best of luck with your presentation!" He waved good-bye as he bounded up the steps in front of us into the huge auditorium.

"Come on, let's follow him!" I shouted as we picked ourselves up off the ground, but by the time we had opened the thick wooden door at the top of the stairs, he had vanished. With no idea where to go, we raced down the longest, tallest hallway

I had ever seen in my life, the sounds of
our clattering footsteps echoing all around.
The walls on either side were adorned with
huge oil paintings of cranky-looking old
men staring down at us. Beneath them stood
imposing knight statues. They didn't look like
brave, noble knights, either—more like the
kind that would chop off your head with their
sword just for the fun of it.

Eventually, we reached the end of the
hallway. We looked left, then right. Both
directions offered more of the same—
hallways trailing off into the distance with no
hint of which was the correct path.

"Where now?" asked Jayden.

"I dunno," I said. "I've never been here,
have I?"

"Shhh," said Min. "Do you hear that?"

"Hear what?" asked Jayden.

I was thinking the same thing when I

heard the sound myself. "It's like a sniffing sound," I said.

"Like someone crying," said Jayden, hearing it, too.

"Let's follow it," suggested Min. We dashed off down the hallway to our left, barging through a set of double doors, and immediately saw where the sniffing was coming from. A girl was sitting crying on a bench halfway along the hallway, clutching a fishing rod in her arms. She wore thick, round glasses and looked much younger than me— six or seven years old, maybe. Roger was there, too, his hand on her shoulder.

"There, there, Emily," he said in a comforting voice. "It'll be all right."

"What happened?" I asked.

"That awful Toby Bloom happened, that's what," said Roger. "He's gone too far this time. No one makes my little sister cry."

The girl squinted at us through her tear-soaked glasses, trying to see our faces. Realizing it was no use, she took the glasses off and wiped them on the sleeve of her blazer before putting them back on.

"Everything was going so well," she sobbed. "I was telling everyone about how good my fishing rod is and all the different fish I've caught with it and then suddenly, Toby just stands up and starts shouting 'BOOO-RING!' at me. And then all his horrible friends joined in."

"He always ruins show-and-tell," said Roger. "Always turns it into a contest."

"Toby told me that the whole school was like that," I said.

"No," said the girl. "It's just him and his friends. No one else really cares what other people bring, but he always has to have the best thing. And he always has to make everyone else feel bad about their stuff."

"Don't any of the teachers scold him?" asked Min.

Roger and his sister started laughing. "Not likely," said Roger. "Mr. Farnsworth runs show-

and-tell. He's horrible, and he lets Toby and his friends get away with anything. Honestly, you've never met such an awful teacher."

I was just about to tell him I might know someone worse when there was a burst of static from my pocket.

"Eric…. ERIC!" shouted Pan.

"Pan," I said, turning away from Roger and Emily so they wouldn't hear. "We're in the building. We're just trying to figure out how to get you out of there."

"Well, figure it out quickly," said Pan. "Toby's up soon. Mini-Dragons are excellent at remaining calm, but even we have our limits!"

"Okay, okay, sit tight," I said. I turned to Roger and Emily. "Where's show-and-tell happening?"

They both pointed a little way farther down the hall to a set of glass doors.

WELCOME TO LA-DI-DA LAND

We took off and peered inside. It was a concert hall, with a balcony and everything, although there didn't seem to be anyone up there at the moment. Hundreds of students were watching the stage, where a boy about my age was showing off a radio-controlled teddy bear to a chorus of loud boos.

Toby sat in the back of the hall, a smug look on his face as he and a small group of boys heckled the boy onstage. My backpack lay on the seat next to him, and I thought I could almost make out two black eyes peeking through a small unzipped gap.

We couldn't just barge in and grab the bag. Not with everyone there.

Min's face lit up.

She walked back over to Emily, who was still sitting on the bench. "How good at fishing are you?"

"She's the best!" said Roger.

Emily nodded. "I *am* pretty good."

"What would you say," Min said, "if I told you there was a way you could get back at Toby, right now?"

Emily's tears dried up in an instant, and an unmistakable glint appeared in her eye. "I'd say, 'What are we waiting for?'"

CHAPTER 7
FISHING FOR DRAGONS

"Left a little … right a little … right a little more…."

If you've ever played one of those games at the arcade where you try to pick up a stuffed toy with a tiny crane, then you'll know what this was like. Except with a fishing rod instead of a crane and a Mini-Dragon as the prize.

From the balcony, the three of us could only watch—and hope that Emily was as good at fishing as she claimed.

With Toby's bag—the one he swapped

for mine—attached to the end of the line, she gently let out the reel, lowering the backpack slowly toward where Toby was sitting.

"Can't you go any faster?" asked Jayden.

"If I go too fast the line could snap, and the bag might drop onto Toby's head," said Emily.

"I don't see the problem with that," said Jayden.

"The problem is we won't get Pan back," I whispered.

"And we'll blow our cover," said Min.

"And it'll ruin my fishing line," said Emily.

"All right, all right," said Jayden. "I was just trying to diffuse the tension a little."

Jayden was right. It *was* tense up there. We were lucky that Toby was sitting right in the back of the hall, so nobody could see the backpack slowly descending from the balcony. As long as no one looked up, the only person likely to catch us at that moment was the blond-haired boy standing onstage, clutching a large, cool-looking bone.

"A bone?" heckled Toby. "Booo-ring!"

"It's from a *Tyrannosaurus rex*," said the boy, his voice wavering. "My mom's a paleontologist, and she swiped it from her

94

job just so I could show it to you. It's millions of years old."

"Yuck!" said Toby, holding his nose. "Gross! I wouldn't feed that to my dog." Laughter broke out among the kids sitting closest to Toby, who were treating him like he was the funniest person ever.

"He doesn't even have a dog," I muttered. "He's allergic to them."

It was clear Roger was right, despite what Toby had claimed—show-and-tell was cruel because of him, not everyone else.

"Eric, what's happening?" said Pan, the walkie-talkie in my hand crackling to life.

I turned away from Emily. "Pan, we're almost there. We just need Roger to do his thing."

"Who's Roger?" said Pan. "Never mind; just hurry. I'm not sure what's worse—being stuck in this bag or having to listen to Toby all day. Actually, I *am* sure. It's the second one."

"Who are you talking to?" asked Emily, squinting at me suspiciously through her glasses.

"That's Pan," said Min, before I could reply. She took a deep breath then added, "He's a miniature dragon from China whose parents shipped him off to live in Mexico with his aunt and uncle in a box of bean sprouts, but who accidentally ended up at my parents' restaurant and was then delivered in a takeout box by me to Eric who then befriended him, but Toby, who is Eric's neighbor, thinks he's a super-advanced toy and keeps trying to steal him."

As Min took a large gulp of air, Jayden and I looked at each other, then at Emily, who was looking at Min.

Emily rolled her eyes. "Fine, don't tell me

then," she said, before turning back to the fishing line. "Okay, we're there."

We watched as Roger, right on cue, made his way along the row to where Toby's bag dangled next to mine. In one deft motion, he switched the hook from one bag to the other and gave the fishing line a gentle tug to let his sister know that the deed was done.

As Emily began to reel in my bag, I realized that the boy onstage, still being heckled for his awesome dinosaur bone, was watching us with a curious expression on his face. He couldn't know what we were up to exactly, but he seemed to understand that it wasn't going to be good for Toby. Smiling to himself, he walked offstage.

A bored-looking man sitting in the front row stood up. He wore a black gown and one of those mortar-board hats from olden times.

"Yes, *thank you* for that, Peter," he said

in a snooty voice. "Next time if you could at least *try* to bring in something interesting, it would be appreciated. Onto our final presentation for today, which I have been assured is worth the wait. I can't imagine it could be *less* interesting than the things we've seen so far, but with you all involved, who knows? Anyway, without further ado, Toby Bloom."

Toby jumped up from his chair, grabbed his bag, then began strutting down the hall like he owned the place.

At that moment, Emily pulled my bag over the top of the balcony.

"Here you go," she said, handing it to me before rushing toward the staircase.

"Where are you going?" asked Min.

"I don't know what's in that bag we just gave Toby," she said, "but I do know I want to have a good seat for when he opens it."

FISHING FOR DRAGONS

Before we could even thank her, Emily was gone.

I unzipped my bag, and Pan sprang onto my shoulder. His eyes were a bit bleary, and his face looked a paler shade of green than usual, and yet I had never seen him look so relieved. I knew the feeling.

"Eric!" he shouted. "You did it."

"No, *we* did it," I said, looking at the others.

"No, *they* did it," said Jayden, pointing down to Emily and Roger, who had found a couple of seats near the front.

"We haven't done anything yet," said Min sternly. "We still have to get back to school."

Min was right. The Deerfield Dragons wouldn't finish their game for a while—we'd have to find another way to travel across town. There were only 20 minutes until lunch was over. And we had to hope that Miss Biggs was still catching up on her much-needed beauty sleep.

Even so, there was no way we could leave just yet. It was about to get interesting.

Toby had already opened his bag onstage and was frantically fumbling around inside. I could see that panic was starting to set in as it dawned on him that he was missing a dragon. His face had turned a bright shade of red, a mix of embarrassment and anger.

"Come on, Bloom!" barked the teacher. "We haven't got all day. What's this impressive thing that you've been bragging about to everyone?"

Toby's mouth opened and closed a few times. "Um … yeah … sorry, Mr. Farnsworth…. Uh, yeah, here it is." He took out a book from his bag and held it up.

Complete silence.

"A *book*?" shouted a boy. "That's it?"

"Um … yeah," said Toby, reading the cover. "Charles Dickens. *Great Expectations*. It's really old and stuff."

"Older than a dinosaur bone?" Percy shouted out.

"Well … no … at least, I don't think it is," said Toby. "It's expensive, though.…"

"I can download it on my phone for free!"

shouted someone in the back.

"Yeah, and your phone doesn't weigh a ton," came another voice. "Plus it has games. What games do you get with your book?"

"Well … none," said Toby. "It's a book."

By this time an excited Mr. Farnsworth had bounded onto the stage. "Quiet, everyone. Bloom, is that a first edition?"

Toby nodded. "Yes, sir. My dad got it."

"May I?" asked Mr. Farnsworth, his hands shaking in anticipation.

Toby handed him the book.

Mr. Farnsworth held the book as if it were a newborn baby. His face beaming with joy, he gently opened the cover.

The four of us sighed at the same time. After all that, Toby was somehow still going to come out of this smelling of roses.

But then, moments later, Mr. Farnsworth's face dropped.

He slammed the book shut and tossed it carelessly back to Toby. "Your father's been conned. This is a *second* edition."

Toby looked crestfallen. "But … but … it's still really old," he said.

Mr. Farnsworth didn't seem to care. "Yet another disappointment," he said curtly. "I'm going to lunch." With that, he left the hall.

As laughter broke out, the four of us looked at each other. Even though Toby had given out much worse to the other kids, it wasn't any fun watching him get humiliated. Without speaking a word, we headed toward the staircase. I took one last look at Toby.

And Toby looked back at me. His mouth hanging open, he rubbed his eyes as if he couldn't believe what he was seeing. Next, his eyes drifted to my backpack. He looked down at his own backpack, and you could almost see the gears turning in his head as he tried to put together what had happened. Then it dawned on him.

Let's just say that if he had looked angry before, it was nothing compared to now.

CHAPTER 8
SHOWDOWN

Bundling Pan into my bag, I sprinted down the stairs with Min and Jayden. Moments later, Toby's voice rang out in the hallway.

"There they are! *Get them!*"

I glanced back as three other boys gave chase. Each one was almost twice the size of Toby—well, in height at least.

"I should have known Toby would have henchmen!" shouted Jayden.

"He does seem the type, doesn't he?" agreed Min. "Uh … where are we going?"

As we ran down an unfamiliar hallway, I

realized that we must have taken a wrong turn, but since there were now three huge Toby-Guards storming toward us, turning back wasn't really an option. We had no choice but to keep going.

We took a left down another long hallway filled with yet more suits of armor and even more miserable old men staring down at us.

"I think we're lost," I gasped.

"I know the way," said Pan, popping his head out of my backpack.

"How?" I asked, looking over my shoulder. "You were in the bag the whole time."

"Yes, but you're forgetting that Mini-Dragons are excellent navigators," he said. "We have almost a sixth sense for finding places. You need it for living in the mountains because all the rocks look the same."

"So navigate!" cried Jayden.

"All right," said Pan. "Turn left here."

"Then right," he said.

"Another right," he continued.

"Then right again," he said. "There. You should be outside now."

We found ourselves right back where we'd started, Toby-Guards closing in fast.

"That's weird," said Pan. "I was sure that was the way. Do you think they could have changed it?"

"In the time we've been running?" I asked.

"Yes."

I closed my eyes. "No, Pan. Do you think …. I don't know, that maybe you're NOT a good navigator?"

Pan considered this for a second before shaking his head. "That doesn't sound very likely."

I let out a groan. According to the *Encyclopaedia Dragonica*, Mini-Dragons are the most stubborn of all the dragons. They definitely had that right. There was no time to argue with him though—we had to get going before...

....we ran into Toby.

"That's ... far ... enough," gasped an extremely out-of-breath Toby.

We turned to run back the way we had just come, only to find Toby's goons blocking our path.

"Eric, meet my associates," said Toby. "Big Ricky, Big Quinn, and Big Joey."

Jayden and Min looked at each other. "I also thought he'd be the type of kid to call his friends associates," said Jayden.

Min nodded. "They're probably *really* thick, too. Henchmen are always really thick."

Big Ricky laughed and pointed at the other two. "Ha. She just called you guys thick."

"No," said Big Joey. "She called *you two* thick."

SHOWDOWN

"She called all three of you thick," snapped an exasperated Toby. "Ugh! You're *so* thick. Will you just get the bag already?"

Grumbling, the three of them took a step toward us.

That was as far as they got. A small hook flew through the air, connecting itself to the back of Big Ricky's blazer. As he turned to see what it was, the line yanked backward.

Big Quinn moved to help his friend and went flying in the process, tripping over an inconveniently placed remote-controlled teddy bear.

Big Joey found his path blocked entirely by an extremely irate-looking Peter wielding a *Tyrannosaurus rex* bone.

Roger stepped in front of Toby. "Leave them alone," he said.

Ignoring him, Toby lunged toward me, before Roger grabbed him and pulled him back. "But ... but ... they're not even from this school!" shouted Toby.

Roger looked at us.

I nodded. "It's true," I said.

"Well, that explains your funny outfits," said Roger.

I could see Jayden frowning, but he didn't say anything.

"We had to come here because Toby took

something that didn't belong to him," I said.
"But now we need to get back to our own
school."

"Which is all the way across town,"
added Min with a groan.

Roger smiled at us. "I might be able to
help you with that," he said.

He reached into his pocket and took out a
set of keys.

CHAPTER 9
THE RETURN TRIP

"You know, they're not *all* like Toby after all," noted Jayden when we got outside. "Though their uniforms are still bonkers."

"Are you sure you know what you're doing?" I asked Jayden, who had insisted on taking the keys.

"Of course," he replied. "Jaydens are excellent at driving golf carts."

"Even if we get to school in one piece," said Min, "has anyone thought about what we do with the golf cart afterward?"

"One problem at a time," said Jayden.

It wasn't like we had any better options, so we climbed back into Roger's cart. Pan slipped out of my bag onto my lap.

"I'm not missing this," he said with a grin.

Jayden inserted the key into the ignition and turned it. The cart roared like a bear being woken from its slumber.

"Seat belts on, everyone," said Jayden. "It's time to see what this baby can do."

As we buckled up, Jayden grabbed the steering wheel and slammed his foot down on the pedal.

Slowly, we started to move backward. Unimpressed, Pan, Min, and I glared at Jayden.

"Whoops," he said, blushing. He tried the next pedal. We stopped moving slowly backward and began moving slowly forward. "That's better."

"It's not *that* much better," said Min.

"Min's right," I said. "Roger drove it much faster."

"Okay, okay," said Jayden, sounding annoyed. "Let me see.…" He pressed a button next to the steering wheel, and the cart shot forward. Even so, it wasn't fast enough. I checked my watch—we had 10 minutes to get across town.

"I could take a look at it," offered Pan.

"NO!" the three of us shouted at once. When Pan had taken it upon himself to tinker with my electric scooter, Toby had ended up stuck in an apple tree.

Pan rolled his eyes. "Not the tree thing again? I still don't see what the fuss was about. They had him down within a couple of hours. And anyway, I know where I went wrong now, so it definitely wouldn't happen again."

"*Definitely* wouldn't happen again?" I said.

"*Probably* definitely," said Pan.

"You're not exactly filling us with confidence," said Min.

"We have no choice," I said. "All right, Pan, go for it."

Jayden stopped the cart as Pan rubbed his tiny claws together with glee before sliding down into the front beneath the steering wheel. He sliced open a plastic panel beneath it and then disappeared into the opening. Jayden, Min, and I waited with bated breath as we listened to the muffled sounds coming from within the cart.

Pan reappeared from the gap and sat
back on my lap. "Okay, try it now," he said.
Jayden turned the key and then:

BOOOOOOOOOOOOM!!!!

THE RETURN TRIP

The cart rocketed down the path and out onto the street. Min and I clutched our seats for dear life while Jayden did the same to the steering wheel and Pan did the same to my leg. We were speeding down the road, flying past cars and pedestrians.

Actually, we were about to run out of road.

"Hold on!" shouted Jayden, as if we weren't already doing that. He turned the wheel to the left. The cart screeched against the pavement as it rotated, the sudden change of direction causing the right side of the vehicle to lift off the ground so that we were turning on two wheels. Just when it seemed like we might topple over completely, the cart dropped back down, and we shot off again.

"We need to get off this road!" shouted Min.

Jayden grinned. "I know a shortcut."

I already knew what Jayden was talking about. Evergreen Park was right ahead. It could work.

You'd think driving through traffic in a dragon-modified golf cart would be scary enough, and it was, but moments later, I saw something genuinely terrifying.

Mom's car. As I looked into the back window, Posy smiled at me, waving furiously.

THE RETURN TRIP

Mom hadn't noticed; she was too busy watching the road in front of her. I could see Posy trying to get her attention. If my sister had been able to talk in a language that wasn't mostly wailing random words, we would have been done for, but Mom didn't seem to be taking her seriously. Then Mom's head started to turn....

Luckily, at that moment, Jayden slammed the steering wheel to the left and turned off toward Evergreen Park, leaving the road, and Mom, behind. We hurtled through the park. It only took a few minutes to get to the other end, but in that time we had:

Ruined four picnics.

Accidentally scored a goal in a soccer game.

Caught two balls.

Been chased by eight dogs.

Almost knocked over a dozen joggers.

Successfully jumped one small duck pond.

We burst out of the park gates and onto Deerfield Road. The school was now within sight. Jayden put his foot down on the brake, causing the cart to screech all the way along the road until we came to a stop outside the school gates.

Pan climbed up my arm and slid into my bag as I undid my seat belt and jumped out.

"Good luck!" shouted Min and Jayden as I sprinted into school. I bolted down the hallway toward our classroom and stopped outside the door.

"Well, here we are," I said.

Pan popped his head out of the bag. "Thanks for coming to get me," he said. "I'm sorry I was so much trouble."

"It wasn't your fault, Pan," I said. "And we couldn't just leave you with Toby, could we?"

"I guess not," said Pan. "You know, it's kind of silly, but for a minute I did wonder what it would be like if Toby showed me to everyone."

"I don't think it would have ended well," I said.

"I know," said Pan. "I guess I just liked the idea of being involved. I think that's really why I wanted to come to school with you in the first place."

I smiled. "Pan.... I wasn't going to tell you this until later...," I said. "But I *did* have a plan to involve you in *our* show-and-tell that wouldn't risk you getting taken away. And if by some miracle I'm still alive this afternoon, then I promise you'll be a part of it."

"How?" he asked.

I unzipped the front pocket of my bag enough for Pan to see what was inside. His tiny eyes lit up with excitement.

"But ... but ... I don't understand," he said.

"I'll explain later," I said. "But now you

need to get out of sight."

Pan nodded and dropped back into the bag, but not before giving my hand a hug.

Then I opened the door and stepped into the classroom.

Miss Biggs was nowhere to be seen.

Suddenly, the door slammed shut behind me. I spun around and there she was, grinning that horrible, cruel grin of hers.

"Welcome back, Crisp."

CHAPTER 10
ROAR AND TELL

"You're in for it now, sunshine," said Miss Biggs, walking over to her desk.

I was gutted. It felt like I had just run a marathon only to trip and break my leg at the finishing line. It wasn't so much the fear of what Miss Biggs would do that bothered me; it was the annoyance of coming so close, only to fail right at the end.

Actually, no, I take that back. The fear of what Miss Biggs would do to me was definitely worse.

"Please, Miss Biggs, I can explain," I

said in a panicked voice. I mean, *obviously*
I couldn't explain, but that's what people
say in moments like these, isn't it? My brain
scrambled for a plausible excuse:

1. I was kidnapped by aliens.

2. I accidentally fell into a wormhole to another dimension.

3. The FBI took me in for questioning, believing me to be an international spy.

4. I had to rescue a Mini-Dragon.

That last one just sounded ridiculous.

Luckily, Miss Biggs wasn't interested in
hearing excuses.

"I'm not interested in hearing excuses,"
she said. "It's curtains for you, Crisp. And not
nice curtains, either. Horrible, thick, burgundy
curtains that shut out the light. You'll be doing
detention until you're 50 for this."

As I mentioned earlier, when you think a

situation involving Miss Biggs can't get any worse, it does.

Suddenly, the zipper on my bag opened, and a furious-looking Pan jumped out and landed on Miss Biggs's desk. I froze, like a Mini-Dragon sensing danger.

"That's it, Biggs! I've had it up to here with you!" shouted Pan, holding a claw about 6 inches above the desk. "All Eric was doing was helping his friend get out of trouble. You need to lighten up, lady. You're supposed to be a teacher, not a prison guard—why don't you try actually teaching for once, instead of making everyone's life miserable? Oh, yeah, and his name is Eric, not Crisp—you're as bad as that horrible Toby!"

Miss Biggs stared open-mouthed at Pan for a few seconds before letting out an ear-piercing shriek and then fainting into her chair.

Pan and I looked at each other.

He coughed. "I probably shouldn't have done that, huh?"

"Probably not," I agreed, too stunned to get upset.

Then a crazy idea entered my head.

The sound of the bell ringing woke Miss Biggs up, jolting her to life. I looked up calmly from my desk.

"Everything all right, Miss Biggs?" I asked innocently.

She looked nervously around the room. "Wh-wh-where is it?" she asked.

"Oh, it's right here," I said, lifting up the report from my desk. The one that Pan had written the night before.

"No," she said shaking her head, "not that, I mean.... Wait, you finished the report?"

"Of course, Miss Biggs," I said. "I finished it a while ago, but I didn't want to wake you."

"But how could you have?" she said, looking confused. "You weren't even here!"

I gave her a puzzled look. "I've been here all through lunch, Miss Biggs."

By now, kids were filing into the classroom, Min and Jayden among them.

"No, you haven't," she said, her voice getting higher. "You left.... And then you came back, and I scolded you.... And then a tiny dragon started yelling at me."

The class fell silent as everyone looked at Miss Biggs.

"A dragon, Miss Biggs?" I asked in a low voice.

"Yes! It was ... it was *little*...."

"A *Mini*-Dragon, Miss Biggs?" asked Min. Jayden stifled a giggle.

"Well … I mean … that is…," said Miss Biggs, scratching her head.

"Are you sure it wasn't just a dream you were having, Miss Biggs?" I said, trying to sound helpful.

Miss Biggs considered this. "I.… I suppose that does make more sense.… I mean, well, there's no such thing as dragons … is there?"

"I don't think so, Miss Biggs," I said.

She nodded slowly. "Right … right. Well, it must have been a dream then. And you definitely didn't sneak out?"

"No, Miss Biggs," I said, approaching her desk and handing her my report. "If I hadn't been here, I wouldn't have had time to finish this."

She looked blankly at the report. "No,"

she said slowly. "That's true. Yes … a
dream. It must have been a dream. Thank
you, *Eric*."

Every head in the classroom turned from
Miss Biggs to me.

If I had to guess why, I'd say it was
probably because none of them could
remember Miss Biggs ever calling someone
by their first name.

Later that afternoon, Min, Jayden, and I were
giving our presentation for show-and-tell.
We were the last ones up, and by that time,
fatigue had set in throughout the class. It was
almost time to go home, and everyone just
wanted the bell to hurry up and put them out
of their misery. Even Jayden getting inside
a cupboard and Min radioing in from the
hallway wasn't enough to get anyone to take

their eyes off the clock. But we had a plan to win them back.

"We use the walkie-talkies mostly to talk to each other," I said, standing at the front of the class, "but every now and then, we pick up transmissions from other people, too."

"From all over the place," added Min, still outside the room.

A few pairs of eyes drifted from the clock to look at us doubtfully.

"Really?" said Miss Biggs, who had been a bit distracted ever since lunch, but now seemed to be giving us her full attention. "Show us, then."

"Um … well, it doesn't always work, you see," I said.

"There's always an excuse with you, isn't there?" she said dryly.

"…Hello?" said Pan.

Miss Biggs's jaw dropped to the floor.

"Hello?" I said, pretending to look surprised. "Who is this?"

"My name's Pan. Who is this?"

"My name's Eric," I said. "I'm in the middle of a show-and-tell."

"Nice. How's it going?" asked Pan.

"Much better," I said, as all eyes in the room were now on me.

"Where are you from, Pan?" asked Jayden from the cupboard.

"China," he replied.

"Me, too," said Min. "Well, my mom and dad are, anyway."

"But I live in the United States now," continued Pan. "It's wonderful! I've got the greatest friends in the whole world. They're the reason I'm talking to you now. You see, I found out today that they all chipped in their allowance money and bought me my very own walkie-talkie."

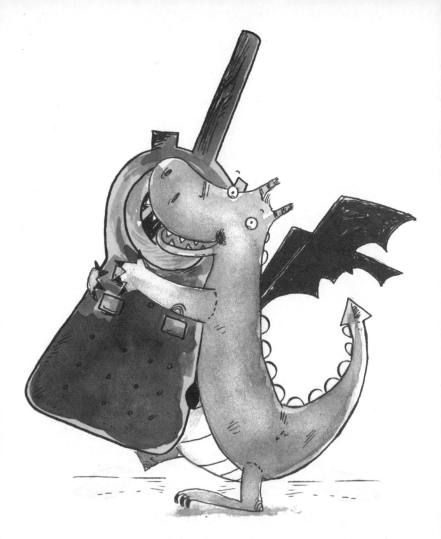

"Wow," said Jayden. "They sound pretty awesome."

"They are," said Pan.

It had taken a couple of weeks for the

three of us to save up for the fourth walkie-talkie. Dad had only picked it up for me yesterday—I told him mine was broken. We had been planning on giving it to Pan when we were all together, but today seemed as good a time as any. From the comfort of my backpack, on the back of my chair, Pan got to be part of a show-and-tell after all.

Miss Biggs had stood up and was slowly crossing the room toward us.

"That voice...," she said. "I know it from somewhere...."

"Anyway ... I, um ... need to be going now," said Pan, obviously sensing trouble. "Good luck with your talk."

"'Bye," said the three of us.

"No, wait!" cried Miss Biggs, but Pan was gone.

Miss Biggs stared at us. "It *was* a dream ... wasn't it?" she muttered, almost to herself.

Then something caught her eye through the window. We looked out to see a golf cart being hauled away by a tow truck.

Miss Biggs shook her head. "I need a vacation."

At that moment, finally, the bell rang.

"How was your day, dear?" asked Mom as we drove home. "Anything exciting happen?"

I felt a surge of panic—had Mom seen us in the golf cart at lunchtime? "No," I said quietly.

"Well, that's not true, is it?" she said.

I gulped. "W-w-what do you mean?" I asked.

"Toby's school," she said.

My heart sank. She knew. We had almost gotten away with it. *Almost.*

"I can explain," I said, playing nervously with the walkie-talkie I still had in my hand.

"Oh, there's no need for that," she said. "I know all about it."

"You do?"

"Oh, yes. I was talking to Mr. Waller before you arrived," she said. "He was telling me all about the Deerfield Dragons crushing La-Di-Da 49–0."

I almost melted into my seat with relief.

"Probably best we don't mention it to Toby, though," said Mom, giving me a wink in the rearview mirror.

"No," I said, laughing. "I won't."

"It was quite funny today, actually," said Mom. "We were just on our way back from Posy's preschool when she started saying your name over and over again. I think she must have seen someone who looked like you."

I rubbed the back of my neck nervously. "Ha! Yeah, she must have."

As Mom switched on her awful show tunes, my walkie-talkie crackled into life.

"Hey, it's me," whispered Pan.

"Can this wait?" I said as quietly as I could.

"It won't take long," he said.

"Okay, quickly," I said.

"I was just wondering where we stood with me coming with you to school tomorrow?"

I stared at the walkie-talkie, speechless. There was only one possible answer to a question like that.

I clicked the walkie-talkie off.

**Bursting for more?
Here's a sneak peek of Eric
and Pan's next adventure....**

CHAPTER 1
PAN THE PARTY PLANNER

"Echo-Romeo-India-Charlie, I have eyes on the objective. The chickens are in the henhouse. I repeat, the chickens are in the henhouse."

I looked blankly at the walkie-talkie in my hand. We didn't have a henhouse. Or chickens. I clicked the button to talk. "Pan, what are you talking about?" I asked.

Even above the noise of all the people gathered behind me in my living room, I could hear Pan sighing on the other end. "It's code, Eric," he said. "Honestly, are

Mini-Dragons the only ones who know how to use walkie-talkies properly?"

"No, but not everyone gets to hang around the house all day learning stuff from old cop movies," I said.

"Fine. The message is: your parents are here," he said. "And now that I've finished being the lookout, can I come downstairs?"

"In a couple of minutes," I said. "Come down once they're inside. I'll meet you in the hall, and then you can hide in my pocket."

"Ah, the glamorous life of a Mini-Dragon," said Pan.

I turned to face the room. "All right, everyone, it's time!" I shouted before switching off the lights.

There was silence, followed by the sound of the front door opening, footsteps walking through the hall, the opening of the door, the clicking of the light switch, then:

"SURPRISE!!"

"Ahhhhhhhhhh!!!" screamed Mom.

"Ahhhhhhhhhh!!!" screamed Dad.

"Mom, Dad, relax! It's okay!" I said.

"Eric?" said Mom, her fright turning to confusion. "What is all this?"

I glanced back at the dozens of people in our living room wearing party hats, the balloons scattered everywhere, the brightly colored gift boxes piled in a corner, and the huge "Happy Anniversary" banner draped from the ceiling.

I thought it was kind of obvious.

"It's a surprise party," I said.

"Oh, right," said Mom, nodding slowly. "For who?"

I slapped my forehead. "For you and Dad, of course. Happy 20th wedding anniversary!"

"HAPPY ANNIVERSARY!" bellowed everyone behind me.

My parents stared at each other in shock.

"Well," said Dad. "It's certainly a surprise."

"You have Eric to thank for that," said Aunt Ruth, appearing next to me. She had been taking care of us while Mom and Dad were out. "Organized the whole thing himself."

My parents' heads turned sharply back toward me. They looked even more surprised than before.

"This was all you?" asked Dad, unable to hide the doubt in his voice.

He was right to be doubtful, of course. I hadn't organized this by myself. In fact, I'd hardly done any of it. I just happened to be good friends with a Mini-Dragon. And Mini-Dragons are excellent at party planning.

The whole idea had been Pan's to begin with. Once he'd found out that my parents' anniversary was coming up, he had been like a Mini-Dragon possessed. I think maybe he wanted to do something nice for them to try and make up for all the trouble he had caused since his arrival. Or maybe it was just because he had enjoyed my last birthday party so much. Now *that* was a good party, although hopefully this time we can avoid firing anyone into a tree on a rocket-powered scooter.

Pan's party planning had consisted of:

- Organizing the catering over the phone. It was a challenge to convince him to order anything other than prawn crackers, though.

- Making all the decorations, although he struggled with the balloons—accidentally blowing fire into them instead of air.

- Making the guest list and sending out invitations to all my parents' friends and family. We had to sneak a look in Mom's journal for their addresses.

- Engineering an elaborate plot where he called up Dad and pretended to be a radio-show host claiming that he had won a free meal at a top restaurant in town. That restaurant was Panda Cottage, the Chinese restaurant that had once delivered Pan to my house inside a box of bean sprouts.

- Our friend Min was able to convince her parents, the owners of said restaurant, to cover the bill. This gave us plenty of time to get everything set up and also allowed Min to tip us off when my parents were leaving.

Of course I could hardly tell my parents that a Mini-Dragon had arranged their party, so I smiled and nodded, taking all the credit.

"But ... how did you afford everything?" said Mom, looking panicked. "Tell me you haven't been using our credit cards!"

"I've not been using your credit cards," I said, rolling my eyes.

"Of course he hasn't, Maya," said Aunt Ruth. "We all chipped in."

"Oh," said Mom. "Well ... I don't know what to say. Thank you, Eric. This is lovely."

I could see her eyes beginning to well up, and I knew what was coming next. She wrapped her arms around me, squeezing me to within an inch of my life, then planted a massive kiss on my face.

"Yeah, nice one, son," said Dad,

punching me affectionately on the arm.

Suddenly, a flash of light almost blinded us.

"Pic-ture," said Posy, my two-and-a-half-year-old sister, wielding her new favorite toy—a kid's camera that Aunt Ruth had bought her.

She was obsessed with it, always popping up when you least expected it to take a photo. It was a bit of a nuisance, especially as I had to check it all the time in case she snapped Pan. Usually it was okay, because Mini-Dragons can freeze themselves if they sense danger, so mostly he just looked like a toy. But she was sneakier than you'd expect a toddler to be, and the camera also had a video mode, so I couldn't take any chances. On this occasion, however, I was more than happy to pose for Posy. She took one of me, Mom, and Dad, and then Aunt Ruth took one of the four of us.

Pictures out of the way, I left my parents to mingle with the rest of our friends and family. The Blooms, our next-door neighbors, had shown up, too. Mr. Bloom was like a bigger version of his son Toby—the same curly hair, the same bright red cheeks, and the same appetite. Together they had taken the buffet table hostage, the pair of them busy stuffing their faces with prawn crackers (well, I had to let Pan order *some*, didn't I?). Mrs. Bloom stood next to them dressed in something my mom called a "Power Suit," which isn't nearly as exciting as it sounds. Unlike her family, Mrs. Bloom showed no interest in the buffet, or anything else for that matter, other than the phone she was tapping away on.

"Mini-Dragons sure know how to throw a party," said Jayden, appearing at my side, with Min.

"Yeah ... they ... sure ... do," she panted. "Sorry ... biked ... over ... here ... as quickly ... as I ... could ... after your ... parents left. Where is ... Pan, anyway?"

"Surely you let him come?" said Jayden. "After he put in so much work?"

"Of course," I said. "As if I could stop him even if I wanted to. He was going to come down and hide in my pocket once my parents arrived. I'll go and get him."

I walked out to the hall, where we'd arranged to meet, but there was no sign of Pan.

"That's weird," I said, stepping back into the living room. "He's not there."

"Give him a shout," suggested Jayden, pointing toward my walkie-talkie.

"Good idea," I said, clicking the call button. "Pan. Are you coming? Pan?"

There was no reply.

The three of us looked at each other with the same anxious expression on our faces. I could tell we were all thinking the same thing. Pan wasn't the type of Mini-Dragon to take his time joining a party. To be honest, I don't know if there *is* a type of Mini-Dragon who likes to take their time, but Pan definitely isn't one of them.

It was time to start worrying.

ABOUT THE AUTHOR

Tom Nicoll has been writing since he was in school, where he enjoyed trying to fit in as much silliness in his essays as he could possibly get away with. When not writing, he enjoys playing video games (especially the ones where he gets beaten by kids half his age from all over the world). He is also a big comedy, TV, and movie nerd. Tom lives just outside Edinburgh, Scotland, with his wife and daughter.

THERE'S A DRAGON IN MY BACKPACK!
is his second book for children.

ABOUT THE ILLUSTRATOR

Sarah Horne grew up in Derbyshire, England, and spent much of her childhood scampering in the nearby fields with a few goats. An illustrator for more than 15 years, she started her illustration career working freelance for newspapers and magazines. When not at her desk, Sarah loves running, painting, photography, cooking, movies, and a good stomp up a hill. She can currently be found giggling under some paper in her London studio.

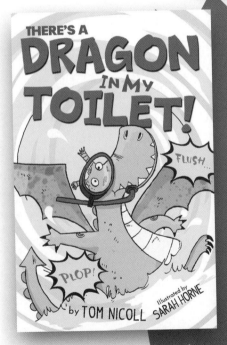